ABOUT A SONG

Guilherme
Karsten

SUBWAY ↓

Dad and I love to
spend time together.

Music is always part of
our adventures.

He says that a song is much
more than just a song.

A song has the power to
brighten our days . . .

. . . and can fly us
to the moon and back.

A song can make us
dance or jump . . .

. . . and even
scream like crazy!

A song reminds us of the
moments that count . . .

. . . and is sometimes
a declaration of love.

A song can reveal our feelings . . .

LOVE
A
NCE
LOVE & P ACE
GIVE A CHANCE to PEACE
love is all you need!
PE

. . . and make us feel that
everything will be all right.

When the melody ends,
it suddenly brings us
back to reality.

That can sometimes
feel confusing . . .

"That's so cool Dad! Now it's my turn
to share my favourite songs with you!"

ABOUT THE SONGS

Did you notice that some of the illustrations in this book refer to a few great musicians? No? They are among my favourite singers, so let me tell you a bit more about them. Let's go!

The lightning, drawn on the rocket, is the hallmark of David Bowie, one of pop music's most experimental and innovative singers. It's a tribute to his song Space Oddity, because every time I hear it, I feel like I am floating in space.

The outfit may look a little bit odd, but if you see someone dressed like this it is probably because they are imitating the king of rock 'n' roll, Elvis Presley. This fellow drove the crowds crazy with his voice and his dances.

I was born in Brazil, and this is my tribute to the "architects" of Brazilian music, Tom Jobim and Vinícius de Moraes, who wrote the song The Girl from Ipanema and made our hearts melt with their beautiful lyrics and melody.

John Lennon and Yoko Ono were known for their political engagement and for promoting peace. If you look closely, you'll also spot the rest of the Beatles in the crowd. My father loved their songs and taught me how to sing them. I'm trying to pass on the same love to my own kids.

This isn't a famous couple, it could be your grandparents singing or playing some songs at home. Do you play any musical instruments, or sing, or just turn up music and dance in your room? If not, I encourage you to sing, dance or play songs with your friends and family. I promise you that these moments will create wonderful memories for you and your loved ones.

ABOUT
THE AUTHOR

← my DAD

← ME

Guilherme Karsten lives in Blumenau, southern Brazil, with his wife and two children. His books are published in several languages around the world. The story of About a Song is very personal. His father loved music and loved to talk about it with his kids, to tell the stories behind the songs and share his favourite bands. His short life was filled with many songs by the artists featured in this book.

Also published by Tate:

ISBN 978 1 84976 710 1

First published 2021 by order of the Tate Trustees by Tate Publishing,
a division of Tate Enterprises Ltd, Millbank, London SW1P 4RG
www.tate.org.uk/publishing

Text and illustrations © 2019 Guilherme Karsten
Original title Una Canción
Translation rights arranged through the VeroK Agency, Barcelona, Spain

A catalogue record for this book is available from the British Library
ISBN 978 1 84976 743 9

Distributed in the United States and Canada by ABRAMS, New York
Library of Congress Control Number applied for

Printed and bound in China by C&C Offset Printing Co., Ltd